Salute

Thomson Burtis

Pharos Books

ISBN: 978-93-67006-91-7
eISBN: 978-93-59838-19-9

Publisher: Pharos Books (P) Ltd.
Plot No.-63, First Floor, Main Mother Dairy Road
Pandav Nagar, East Delhi-110092
Phone: +14049995474, 011-40395855
WhatsApp: +91 9319228272
E-mail: sales@pharosbooks.in
Website: www.pharosbooks.in
Edition: 2024

Printed By: Sushma Book Binding House, Okhla Industrial Area, Phase II, New Delhi-110020

Salute
By : Thomson Burtis

Salute

Before advancing a few choice bits of philosophy, speculation and what have you, I'm going to introduce myself. I do this so that you may promptly divest my theories of any importance whatever, and let them roll off your knife smoothly and without effort. That being done, you can proceed, if you like, to digest the illustrative anecdote concerning the little matter of Lieutenant Percival Enoch O'Reilly, Air Service, Regular Army, versus Lieutenant Ralph Kennedy, Air Service, Reserve Corps.

My name is "Slim" Evans, and I, in an idle moment in 1917, became a member of the Army Air Service. I still am, for the simple reason that I'd have to work twenty hours a day in civilian life to make twenty dollars a week. When I was constructed, the supply of brains, beauty and good sense was very limited. However, there was an overplus of noses and feet, so I turned out six feet five inches tall; thin enough to chase a fugitive collar-button down a drain pipe; and standing in a stooped position on a pair of feet so large that I couldn't fall down if I wanted to.

On the credit side of nigh on to ten years as a flyer, I can put the fact that I've done practically no work, made much more money than I'm worth, have avoided monotony and lived through moments of great excitement, not to say thrills. Furthermore, I've met diversified people and events which, thank God, have kept me from being smug, complacent or bigoted about anything whatever. On the debit side of the ledger, I have only a couple of my own teeth left, and they do not meet; I have a bad left shoulder, three elegant and permanent bumps on my head, and more scars on me than there are on an ice rink after an evening's skating.

With this background, you can attach as much weight as you want to this statement. People who've lived long enough and seen enough to comprehend a little bit of the complexity of human beings and the motives which spur them to their daily performances, will never be too hasty in damning a man to his eternal roast. On the other hand, they'll be very cautious about attaching a pair of wings and a halo to any living human.

Once I did that. Everything was either good or bad, including people. There was no middle ground. As a result of that asinine viewpoint, there are memories that rise and smite me when the wind is in the east. R. E. Morse overtakes me and makes life a hell for hours at a time, as I think back to the dumb, cruel things I've done—and the fact that the same things have been done to me by others doesn't help. Here, a girl I've misjudged; there, a man to whom I've said unwarranted things that I'd give my left hand to take back, and—oh, well, you know, I guess, if you're out of your mental swaddling clothes.

Consequently, there may be some importance to be found in the fact that my own personally buried skeletons fade almost into insignificance before the climax of a situation that I watched on the Rio Grande, in which I, personally, had no part. Furthermore, the things I've seen—gone through, some of them, myself—in ten years of flying become almost like unreal, theatrical claptrap, in comparison with one moment, a mile in the air, that changed a couple of lives and made Penoch O'Reilly into a different man.

You gather, I take it, that the affair made an impression on me.

My observation of the episode started one steaming July morning in McMullen, Texas. Mr. P. Enoch O'Reilly and myself were members, in good standing, of the McMullen flight of the Air Service Border patrol. There were a dozen flights, consisting of ten or twelve flyers and observers, scattered along the Border from Brownsville to San Diego.

The duty of the blithe young men was to pilot DeHaviland airplanes up and down that squirming trouble area, taking peeks at any little matters such as smuggling, rustling, or a little plain and fancy banditing. We aimed to be a sort of Texas Ranger outfit, riding airplanes instead of horses and, in some cases, if I do say it myself, the boys did pretty well. Well enough to make the roar of an airplane motor like the voice of doom to many a frisky outlaw.

Eleven o'clock was the hour for the mail to arrive. I'd just got back from the western patrol to Laredo and stalked into the office with my helmet and goggles still on. It was only a gesture—I never get any mail.

Sitting on the edge of a desk in the operations room, underneath the mailboxes, was Penoch O'Reilly. He was holding a letter in his clenched hand, and his eyes were gazing out of the window with a look in them which was not good to see.

Enthroned in the inner office, at their respective desks, were "Pop" Cravan, our adjutant, and Captain George Kennard, our C. O. Pop was round and obese and bald-headed, with a fiery temper, a nasty tongue, a soft heart and a keen mind.

"Hell!" he snorted loudly. "Another of those reserve officers ordered here for three months active duty at his own request! I suppose he'll crack up three ships and be more trouble than a case of hives."

"Who is he?" demanded the stocky, spike-haired little captain in his raucous voice.

"Name is Ralph Kennedy, and he's a shavetail in the reserve."

"I know him!" barked Penoch O'Reilly suddenly. "Here's a letter from him, in fact."

"Enter into the sanctum, sirrah, and make him known to me," the C. O. invited him spaciously.

Penoch strode in with ludicrously long steps. He was so short that he'd have to stand on a stepladder to kick a duck in the stomach.

I drifted in lazily, but my curiosity was alive. If I wasn't wrong, the look on Penoch's face, as he brooded over that letter, did not indicate ungovernable enthusiasm about the arrival of the new man.

"I knew him a little before the war," O'Reilly stated in that deep bass voice of his.

Coming from his little body, that voice was as surprizing as it would be to get a brass band effect by blowing on a harmonica.

"He's not so bad, I guess. Lived an eventful life, anyhow. Was a sergeant in the Air Service—in my outfit a lot of the time during the war—and learned to fly then. Got a commission in the reserve when the war was over. He's a wonderful mechanic, and he can tell interesting yarns."

"How well can he fly?" demanded Pop truculently. "With these bandits raising hell, and with scarcely enough crates to get flying time in on, we can't afford to let amateurs spread D.H.'s all over the landscape!"

"Pretty good," Penoch admitted grudgingly. "He was an automobile race driver at one time, a trick motorcycle artist at another, and all that."

"Due in this afternoon," remarked Pop, examining the orders in his hand. "Well, I hope he can play bridge."

Penoch's set face relaxed into the ghost of a grin.

"He's pretty good at most card games," he said mysteriously. "Going back to the tents, Slim?"

"Uh-huh. All quiet along the river, Cap."

"I'll go with you," Penoch said evenly, and we marched out.

We were surely a comedy team together; and we frequently were together, because Penoch and I had become close friends as a result of several imbroglios in which we had engaged. He was just an inch over five feet, so you can readily realize that I could have worn the little squirt for a watch-charm.

"Anything special on your mind?" I inquired casually.

"Yeah; but I'll wait until we get to the tent," he told me.

We marched on down the line of buildings that bounded the southern end of the small sandy airdrome. To the east and west were big black corrugated iron hangars, baking in the sun. Northward, a fence was the rim of the field, and a few miles farther north was the rim of one hundred and fifty solid miles of mesquite.

While we are galloping down the line toward the tents, take a look at one of the most amazing chunks of humanity I've ever met. Penoch, as I've said, was short, but his torso was round as a barrel, and his legs straight and thick and sturdy. His muscles, I'd found, were like steel cables, and his strength was as much out of proportion to his size as his voice was.

It was his face, though, that made him prominent in any company. It was square and brown; and a pair of the largest, keenest, brightest blue eyes you ever saw sparkled forth from it and reflected an unquenchable joy in life for its own sake. His hair was red—not pink or sandy or auburn, but red. His eyebrows had been bleached by the sun to a pale yellow; and below his short, turned-up nose, a cocky little mustache, waxed to pin-points, was a similar tint.

His teeth were big and strong and white, and between them, on occasions, there rolled a loud, Rabelaisian "Ho-ho-ho!" that made the welkin ring. Everyone in hearing distance chuckled with him. He looked a bit like a burly little elf—but when he was serious and worried, as he was now, wrinkles leaped into being, and those eyes got hard as diamonds. Then age and experience and hard competence were written for all the world to read.

He is, was, and will be until he dies, one of the most famous characters in the Army. Some of the highlights of his Army career include being stranded in a West Virginia town, where the miners, on strike, were hostile; declaring martial law without authority and running the town for thirteen days, until he could get out; being captured in the Philippines by hostile Moros, given up for lost, and finally returning, safe and sound, an honorary chieftain of the tribe; and numberless other accomplishments of renown. He had been court-martialed a hundred times, due to his peculiar sense of humor, and had always been acquitted, because a board of officers who've laughed steadily for hours at the testimony can't get tough.

Incidentally, he usually hauled his friends into any trouble which he found for himself. I myself had been court-martialed, along with him and Charley De Shields, just a month before. All due to his funny ideas. It gives a little sidelight on a man who is tough to describe, so I'll tell it.

The three of us were in San Antonio on a week-end leave, and at one in the morning we were a bit tight, so to speak. Penoch called up a couple of girls for the purpose of throwing a roadhouse dance party. Being respectable young ladies and in bed, they haughtily bawled him out for calling at such an hour. That made Penoch decide upon vengeance. Charley De Shields is just as nutty as Penoch, and I'm no paragon of dignity.

It was Penoch's idea, though. The apartment house was a small one, in a quiet section of town, and it boasted a small, cozily furnished lobby. We proceeded to divest that lobby of all its furniture. When we finished, we had chairs on top of Charley's sedan, a davenport on the hood, and everything from potted palms to rugs and bric-a-brac inside the car. The lobby was furnished with a telephone, when we left.

Out at Donovan Field we rang the doorbells of our friends, presenting each one with a tasty bit of house-furnishing, as a token of esteem. At five in the morning we retired, to be awakened at two in the afternoon by the news that the owner of the apartment house was after our scalps, and that returning the furniture might knock off a couple of years from our sentences.

We'd forgotten just where we'd left the stuff. However, we secured a big truck and went from house to house, collecting. At dark we set forth for town, between cheering lines of unregenerate flyers. Penoch was on the front seat, clasping a large and ornate vase lovingly, to keep it from breaking. Artificial flowers were in his other hand. Charley tended three standing lamps carefully in the body of the truck and I, at the rear end, blushingly chaperoned a frail chair of the vintage of Louis Quinze, a plant in a glass container, and three spittoons.

Perhaps I shouldn't have mentioned it; but that was Penoch. He radiated more energy than his weight in radium; he could fight like three wildcats rolled into one, and he laughed at, and with, life twenty-four hours a day—usually.

Which made his present preoccupation all the more impressive. We said not a word, until we were in my little two-by-four tent.

"Shoot," I commanded, and he set himself for that purpose.

Whenever he had anything of importance to say, he always planted himself with his legs wide apart, as if setting himself against an onslaught, and he talked with his body motionless, except for a stabbing, emphatic finger.

"It's about this bird Ralph Kennedy," he stated, "and I need advice."

This admission from the self-sufficient Penoch was remarkable in itself. It became even more so as I took a good look at his face. It was hard and set, pugnacious jaw outthrust, and his eyes were a curious mixture of cold savagery and dazed bewilderment.

"I guess you didn't exactly shoot your wad to Kennard, then," I said as casually as I could.

"No, I didn't. I never have to any one, except you; and that was because I had to. I'm afraid I've got to now!"

He just clipped those last words off, with snaps of his teeth.

"You know considerable about me," he went on, seeming to plant himself more solidly, as his eyes met mine squarely.

"Not so damn' much," I came back. "You were in France, of course, and left the army to join the Kosciusko squadron in Poland. Then you were an instructor in the Mexican Air Service, and finally got back into the Army and went to the Philippines for two years. Now here you are. That's all I know."

"Well, you know I've got into trouble in my life," he stated. "Anyhow, Slim, I'm up against it now. To make a long story short, I come of a wonderful family, I suppose, but I ran away from home, and between the years of fifteen and twenty went through a sort of hell, I guess. That's when I met this bird Kennedy. He picked me up when I was a starving hobo, and he proceeded to use me for his own purpose. I was valuable to him in a lot of ways. He's a sort of crooked adventurer—or was. But I'll swear I was innocent as a baby at the time!"

"The soup begins to thicken," I said slowly. "Well, what happened? What was his line?"

"The first thing he had me do was go around and place a bunch of punch-boards in saloons in Buffalo," Penoch said in that fog-horn voice of his. "There were two hundred dollars' worth of punches on each board, and the saloon-keeper was to put up a regulation number of cash prizes—so many twenty-dollar bills, so many tens, and so on, totaling two hundred bucks. When the board was punched out, I was to come around and collect ten dollars for the use of it. We furnished a list of prize-winning numbers, a board to exhibit the prizes on and the punchboard itself."

"That seems all right," I told him.

"Sure." For a second his face lightened, and he was the sparkling, zestful boy again. "But Ralph went around to every saloon and punched out all the prize-winning numbers! Ho-ho-ho!"

I had scarcely started laughing, when his face suddenly turned bleak and cold again, and my laugh, somehow, died in my throat.

"I realized later that I'd been an accomplice in a good many things outside of the law—getting him acquainted with people he could fleece, and all that sort of thing. Finally, he worked the old mine salting racket; but, Slim, he worked it on me! I thought the thing was a cinch, and I persuaded two well-off men I'd got to know to invest a lot of money in it. It was a plain swindle—me innocent, and those men are looking for me yet, I guess. Slim, he can blast me right out of the Army and—well, jail's a cinch, I think."

I could understand all the implications in his words. My own life hasn't been so easy. And when a man hits the open road, to lick the world from a standing start, and is thrown with the scum of that same world through necessity, often with starvation stalking at his side, there are bound to be episodes which the smug people of this world, who've never missed a meal or had a fight, think damn one to eternity. There are ghosts in the closet of every wanderer that ever lived.

"You think he's out to do you dirt," I said finally.

"Not exactly. As a matter of fact, Slim, I think he likes me a lot. But he's for Number One all the time. As cold and unmoral a snake of a man as ever breathed. He'd throw his family, if he had one, to the lions to save himself. And from the time he caught up with me, during the war, to the time I got out, he haunted me. He got himself made a sergeant assigned to my outfit. He borrowed my money, made me introduce him to people I didn't want to know him, because I distrusted him; he took it for granted that he could have special privileges. And now that he's found me again, he aims to be a parasite for the rest of his life. I know it!"

"The short and ugly word," I observed casually, "is blackmail. A bullet is a merciful death for one of that stripe."

Penoch's hand stabbed out at me.

"I know it. And yet the man is likable in a lot of ways, as you'll see. Maybe he thinks I owe him plenty. In a lot of ways he defers to me, admires me and likes me. But, as I say, when he gets in any kind of trouble, or wants anything for himself, there isn't a thing in the world as important as himself. He'd loan me money, if he had it, and he'd sell me into jail for five thousand dollars, if he was broke. The only reason in this world that he's coming here is to live off of me. He must be broke, or a fugitive, or something. He'll draw his pay, borrow mine, if he needs it, and never pay it back. He'll take it for granted that I'll do everything in the world for him. If I refuse, he'll use the club he has over me without mercy."

"And he's a reserve officer," I ruminated aloud. "Listen, Penoch. You've got the goods on him. You can plaster him behind the bars. Why not call his hand and take your chances? You were young, innocent—"

"It would kill the folks," O'Reilly said steadily, "and the Army and flying right now means a hell of a lot to me. It's not so easy, Slim."

Which it wasn't, of course.

"Aside from the money angle, Penoch—and say, that needn't be so bad, at that! If that bozo starts to blackmail you out of your dough, there's no reason why 'Tex' MacDowell, 'Sleepy' Spears and myself each can't fix up a bit of a game and get it back from him by fair means or foul. We'll—"

"Won't do, Slim," he told me. "That is, it might, if it was worked cagily. But if he thought for a minute that I'd given him away he'd plaster me to a fare-you-well. And that isn't the worst of it—the money, I mean. He's funny. He's got a hell of a lot of false pride, or maybe he really thinks he's fit to enter any home in the country. He'd just move right in with me, and he'd be so sore he'd never let up on me, if he so much as suspected that I was stalling him off from meeting any of my friends. And there I am! In a position of having to introduce a man I'm not sure won't cheat at cards, make love to a man's wife, or anything else. And if I don't, it's out of the Army in disgrace, and—"

"It's a tough spot," I said unnecessarily, and he stared morosely at me as he said—

"It's no Paradise."

Then his face seemed to harden. It was all in his eyes, and they were bleak and cold.

"But that devil had better not get gay. If worst comes to worst, I'll kick him out of the Army, resign myself, and hit the road."

He sort of grated that out, and I cut in hastily:

"As a matter of fact, he'd better not slip on the cards or the rest of it, or I'll personally get him. He doesn't strike me as any credit to the Army."

"He'll be too smart for that—around the field, anyway. I suppose I'm a coward; but I'll be miserable while he's here. I'm hoping he won't be tempted to do his stuff. Honest, Slim, what do you think? That I'll be a damn' heel to introduce him around? That I ought to give him away to start?"

"No," I told him, after no thought whatever. "Maybe he's reformed. Anybody you introduce him to will be free, white, twenty-one and able to look out for himself. And I see no reason for you to open up a knife, sharpen it and stick it in your own gizzard before it's necessary."

"Well, it won't take long to make it necessary. He'll hang around my neck just once too often."

With that I left him for the bath-house, there to get washed, polished and highly perfumed. During the rest of the day no loud "ho-ho-ho!" rang out over the field. If I had any tendency to forget the situation, Penoch's set face was a constant reminder. Consequently, you won't find it hard to believe that I accepted Penoch's invitation to become a member of the welcoming committee. I accepted agilely, as a matter of fact, and the witching hour of three forty-five found us tooling his dilapidated old roadster down the thronged main street of McMullen, as quietly as a flock of tanks.

McMullen is one of those new, shiny, progressive little Texas cities, where transportation includes cow-ponies and Rolls Royces. It is a mixture of the old and the new. A completely equipped, honest-to-God old cowboy will tie up his horse in front of a store that sells Parisian gowns.

The depot, as always, held a considerable crowd to greet the one daily train from San Antone. No sooner had Penoch guided his panting monster into parking space, and its wheezes and moans died, than a shiny eight-cylinder speedster appeared in the next stall. A feminine voice was yelling:

"Hello, flyers! Who's arriving?"

"Reserve officer; friend of mine," Penoch was forced to say. "How's my secret sorrow?"

"Fine," returned Miss Shirley Curran airily, hopping out of her car and into ours. "Well, I suppose I might as well look him over."

She was nineteen—one of these slightly dizzy, somewhat confusing flappers that senile old men of thirty-odd like myself had a hard time getting used to a few years back. She was slim and thin-faced and good-looking, with boyishly bobbed blond hair, snapping blue eyes, and agile tongue. She was tireless—a slim streak of flame, who could dance all night, ride all day, smoke seven packages of cigarets, and look as fresh as a daisy.

Her dad was a great old Texan, who'd played a lot of poker, drunk a lot of liquor and had been a great ladies' man in his time. She was the apple of his eye—and a good apple, too. She was a pal to many of the flyers; although, for real playmates, she preferred less mature samples of the male sex—college boys and that sort, who could fling a mean hoof.

She chatted along until the train rattled in and Penoch left the car.

"What's the matter with him?" she demanded.

"Just moody, I guess; he gets that way."

"He does not. He's about as moody as our cow."

"Well, you ask him, then," I told her.

As if sensing my own curiosity, she fell silent, and both of us searched the crowd eagerly. We weren't more than thirty feet from the steps of the single battered Pullman, so I could note every line in the face of the man who shook hands so enthusiastically with doughty little Penoch.

That greeting surprized me. Kennedy's eyes were shining; his face held a genial and infectious grin, and I'll swear that it was plain as the nose on my face that he liked Penoch a lot. And Penoch, too, seemed to melt. I guess the memories of a thousand times, good and bad, creates a bond, even between enemies, when they meet after a long separation.

"Isn't he good-looking!" exclaimed Shirley with zest. "That's the cutest mustache!"

And she was right. He was of medium height, dressed in blue serge and a jaunty straw hat. He removed the hat, as they approached the car, talking eagerly. His hair was black as night, wiry and wavy. His eyes were gray or blue, his nose long and straight; the carefully tailored mustache softened a thin mouth. His shoulders were broad, and his body looked as hard as rock.

As they came closer, I had a funny feeling. He fairly radiated personality; but, somehow, in his slightly small, slightly too close together eyes, I thought I could see meanness. Probably it was because of what Penoch had said, but I seemed to see through a shallow layer of geniality and kindness into a man wherein there was neither moral sense nor unselfishness. Just something as cold and impersonal and impregnable as a rock.

As he approached us, his eyes, which I could now distinguish as green, rested continuously on Shirley. If ever I saw bold admiration, I saw it then. There was something coldly appraising in his stare, and an uncanny hypnotic effect. I'll swear I had a job pulling my own optics off his.

I made one or two revisions regarding his personal appearance, too. In the first place, his hair was shot with gray; in the second place, his chin seemed a bit weak; in the third place, he was an attractive man, despite everything.

When Penoch introduced Shirley and me, he bowed low—a bit too low—and said:

"Pleased to meet you both. So the boy's bought himself a buggy, has he? Some car, 'Peewee,' some car!"

He looked it over with a wide grin.

"It didn't go through the war with you, did it?" he inquired, and he chuckled. It was as merry a chuckle as I've ever heard, too.

Every second or two his eyes would flicker to Shirley's, and never did I see her own gaze drop. When she got into her own car, he handed her in with a flourish, then held her hand a little too long, as he stared into her eyes.

"If you—if you aren't all cluttered up with the well known husband or something, I hope I see more of you, pretty lady," he said airily.

Shirley didn't blush so easily, but the man had her on the run. Despite his careful dress and too careful manners, he gave a subtle impression that he was a rough and ready guy at bottom; but one who had a lot of sheer animal power, without much leavening of civilized feeling. And when he stared at you with those green eyes, you forgot, momentarily, that something that I've tried to describe; the cold, diamond-hard core within him, I mean, and that the geniality of him was a reflection from the surface.

"Nothing like starting to get the old hooks in right at the start," he grinned as he got in with us and waved farewell to Shirley. "By the way, Peewee, how's the old heart been doing lately? Any more of the old dents in it?"

"Nary one," responded little Penoch. "Well, how've you been?"

"Neither here nor there. Not so good lately. Right now, if a house and lot could be bought for a nickel, I couldn't buy a doorknob; so I decided to let Uncle Samuel take care of me for a while. Heh-heh-heh!"

When he chuckled like that, you thought of him as a jovial, humorous scoundrel. And before that twenty minute ride was over, he'd told Penoch a couple of yarns about himself, and had O'Reilly in hysterics and me laughing like the devil. I noted, likewise, that he slipped into the "I seen" and "I done" manner of speech. Being grammatical was foreign to him, as was his bowing to a woman. All surface polish, poorly done.

He moved into the flight with a careless confidence that was sublime. At the dinner table, under Penoch's prodding, he talked and talked with agility and abandon. He'd been everywhere and done everything and, as far as I could tell, he'd been a drunkard and a gambler and a Lothario through it all. Whatever business he had afoot rarely interfered with his wassail and debauch.

He could tell a story so vividly, and with such a sense of humor, that one forgot the bad taste it left in the mouth and just capitulated to the bizarre humor of it. Burglars, gangsters, army officers and persons of high degree came casually into his conversation with bewildering effect. To my dying day I'll never forget his story of a one week's job as chauffeur to a certain internationally famous family. Carnival life, race driving, hot political campaigns, the low-down on the underworld of three big cities. Before the evening was over all these things had been touched on; Kennedy was jovially drunk, and the flight had sat at his feet and listened with unflagging interest. Never once did he slip and make himself an actor in an illegal episode; he was the looker-on, although admitting to friendship with many a criminal.

Early the next morning I set off on the western patrol. To make a long story short, I ran into some bandits, held them awhile with my machine-guns, but finally lost them, due to a forced landing that resulted in my absence from McMullen for three days. Finally, with my ship repaired, I flew it back to the airdrome just at dusk. As I sat down to a late and lonely dinner, Penoch came in with that dignified, long-striding gait.

"How's your friend Kennedy?" I asked him promptly.

"Borrowed two hundred bucks for uniforms and such," he boomed crisply, and sat himself down.

I took one look at him; and that was enough.

"You might as well shoot the works. What's he been up to?" I inquired. "First, how do the boys like him?"

"They get a great kick out of him. They know he's not their equal by birth or breeding or anything like that. It's a sort of patronizing friendship, if you get what I mean. That's what he gets from most people, and what he resents most when, if and as he gets hep to it."

I nodded.

"Well, why the woebegone look in your port eye and the stricken stare in the other?" I asked spaciously.

I didn't want to seem too serious about it. He got to his feet and put one foot on a chair.

"Shirley's fallen right into his trap," he barked. "He's got her hooked tighter than Grant had Richmond; and he's got to lay off!"

"Peewee! Where's the boy?"

Penoch's eyes darted to mine, and his face froze.

"Stick around, and you'll see some fun," he barked raucously, and then his voice reverberated thunderously from the rafters.

"In the dining hall! Come in!"

In came Kennedy, resplendent in a uniform as new as the label on a bottle of bootleg whisky. He was washed, polished and highly perfumed, and he looked well.

"'Lo, Slim! Welcome home! Say, Peewee, can you slip me twenty? I'm as flat as near-beer. Until pay-day?"

"No, I can't. I'm broke myself."

Penoch was on his feet, legs wide apart, planted solidly. His barrel-like, little body seemed to stretch, until his clothes were drawn tightly over it, and his mustache was bristling fiercely. His eyes were bright and cold.

"I'm a stranger, almost; how about borrowing it for me?"

"No!"

"What's the matter, kid? Ain't sore, are you?"

Kennedy seemed really hurt and surprized. As a matter of fact, it was as plain to me as anything could be that Kennedy thought as much of Penoch as he did of any living human. He never missed a chance to slide in a statement that Penoch was a great little guy; and the number of tales he recounted that first evening, to prove what a fighter, thinker and all-round champion Penoch was, were numberless.

"Not exactly. But I've got something to say to you, Ralph, and now's the time. First off, Slim, here, and Slim alone, knows the works. Understand?"

"Who told him?"

Kennedy's face was a mask, now, and the eyes of a snake looked into mine, then shifted to Penoch.

"I did."

"Give yourself the best of it?"

There was venom dripping from his tongue when he said that. He backed away slightly, as if fearful of a physical assault.

"What a fine pal you are!" he spat.

"Be that as it may, you listen. You lay off Shirley, Ralph, or I'll have your history published in the paper! I've hinted at it before. Now I tell you!"

Penoch's were blazing into Kennedy's, and his right fist was stabbing the air. He was set for the battle, be the result what it might.

"Just where do you think you'd end up in that case? And where do you come in to criticize anybody else?" sneered Kennedy.

His eyes seemed rat-like then, somehow, as if they were flickering about for an opening for escape.

"For the sake of argument, we'll say nowhere!" Penoch fairly roared. "I've paid your bills and hauled you around, and introduced a man I wasn't sure wouldn't steal family jewelry, to plenty of people. So far, I haven't had anything but worry over it. But this is different."

"So you're pulling the big blackjack, are you? Rough-stuff, huh? Well, I'm pretty good at that myself, Peewee. So you mind your own damn' business—or else—"

Kennedy's eyes were flat and green and cold, his lips drawn back in the suspicion of a smile, and he looked as close to cruelty incarnate as I care to gaze upon. And hard—gosh!

"I'll do no such thing. And you get just exactly three days to wind up your little affair with Shirley, or I start talking. You can start at the same time, and be damned to you! But we'll both go down together, big boy. You'll go down farthest. My resignation'll be in before I start shooting off my mouth; I figure on that."

For a long ten seconds Kennedy's unwinking eyes bored into blazing Penoch's. The indomitable little flyer, as if carved out of granite, stood there and waited. Kennedy threw his cap on the table. His voice softened, and in a wheedling tone he said:

"What's all this about, Penoch? Good lord, boy, don't go off half-cocked. I ain't done nothin' to Shirley or her old man."

"Not yet, maybe! Why she ever fell for you, I don't know; but she has. And if you've got any intentions at all, they're rotten, and I know it. You couldn't marry her if you wanted to, and if you could and did, she'd break her heart in six months. You're a natural born crook and you know it. You're a great guy in some ways; but there isn't one gram of honesty in your whole body. You'll end up broke or in jail, as sure as there's a jail left. You never gave a woman in love with you a square break in your life, or hesitated at getting everything you could out of any man or woman who got in your power.

"And if you think I'm going to be responsible for getting a kid like Shirley into any mess with you, you're crazy! If you get her she'll know what she's getting, and I don't mean maybe. You're no more eligible to wear that uniform or to mix socially with Shirley than I am to be the Grand Gazabo of Guam. Now, by God, you make up your mind. You're going to do one decent thing in your life, and you're going to do it within three days, by wiping Shirley off the slate and staying where you belong. If you don't, you know what I'll do. That goes just exactly as it lays!"

Penoch had been talking in low, deep tones, but every word was like a muffled bullet. When he had finished, a dangerous human being was crouched, figuratively speaking, with his back to the wall. I put in my horn then, having been stricken with an idea.

"Penoch's right, big boy," I told him. "As a matter of fact, why the hesitation? Shirley means nothing to you except a time-passer—a kid like that."

"Is that so? How do you know so much?" he snarled.

His eyes flashed to Penoch's.

"Gone back on me, have you? All right, you lousy little double-crosser. Watch yourself, and plenty! I'll—"

"You'll what?"

O'Reilly had covered the space between them in one bound, like a bounced ball. Suddenly sheer hatred burned from two pairs of eyes. Kennedy licked his lips, and his smile was mirthless and his eyes indescribable.

"I said to watch yourself," he said softly. "I don't like people that talk too much."

"I guess," I interrupted slowly, "that it may be time for me to do some talking."

"Talk all you want to; but you stand the gaff, and don't forget that, Peewee!"

The look he threw over his shoulder, as he walked out, left no doubt about what he meant. O'Reilly's body relaxed slightly, but his face remained set and strained.

"I've always thought," he said slowly, "that there weren't many bozos in the world I'd hate to have as an enemy as much as I would Ralph. And now the wad is shot, Slim. I guess I'm in for it. But what the hell? The fact that I've talked to you will be the last straw, as far as he's concerned. Shirley or no Shirley, he's doing a lot of low and lofty thinking right now. And he'll have a way figured to get even with me, if it takes a year, without hurting himself. Three days from now should be interesting, what? Ho-ho-ho! The skeletons'll be out doing a song and dance for all McMullen to watch, eh?"

Now that the die was cast, Penoch was himself again, daring the world to do its worst. Indomitable, hard-boiled, soft-hearted, he flung his loud, raucous laughter in Kennedy's face, so to speak, challenging him and the universe in general to get him down.

"Why couldn't you have talked quietly to Shirley," I asked him.

"Tried to," he boomed absently. "She wouldn't even listen. She's nuts, I tell you, and the old man likes him. He's given them a long song and dance about his automobile business in Los Angeles, and all that stuff. If I went to the old man and told him, there'd be hell to pay; the truth would come out that I had peached on him, and then my neck would be chopped neatly. Whichever way it's done, there'll be the same result when I expose him. I'm sunk myself."

"Right now," I ruminated, "he may not be satisfied with just smearing your reputation and having you tried for that mine salting business, at that. Struck me he'd love to throttle you."

"I guess he would," Penoch said calmly. "He served five years for manslaughter in Virginia once."

I went to bed early. I hadn't had much sleep for three days, so at ten o'clock in the morning I was still pounding my ear commodiously. I was awakened by long, lean, drawling Tex MacDowell.

"Take a peek at the paper and then arise and shine," he told me. "We start for the Gulf of Mexico in exactly one hour."

One peer at the headlines, that took up half the front page, awakened me as thoroughly as a pail of ice water would have.

"Laguna In Ruins!" the paper screamed in letters big enough to put on a signboard.

Within a moment I had the details. One of those tidal waves, estimated as at least a hundred feet high and two miles in width, had swept in from the Gulf. Doubtless the result of a volcanic eruption on the sea floor. According to the meager reports available, every house, structure and living thing existing in the portion of Laguna, within a half mile of the beach, had been doomed by that vast crush of water. The remainder of the town, back farther from the beach, had been inundated; but houses were standing, and many of the people had escaped alive. The low country—marshy ground, a lot of it, anyway—was under three feet of water, and Laguna, as well as small settlements along the beach, which had likewise been demolished, was a marooned and ruined little city. Telegraph lines down, railroads washed out, telephones useless, and at least one thousand people dead or washed out to sea.

"We go over to patrol the Gulf for survivors," Tex said tersely. "Donovan Field ships will ferry food and water and medical supplies down. We leave in an hour. Get a move on!"

All I could think of, as I made passes at my whiskers and leaped into my clothes and gulped some food was this—how must it feel to look up and see millions of tons of water about to fall on you? A ten foot wave in a storm makes me feel like an ant bucking a steam roller.

Four men were to be left at the field for patrol. Six ships were warming up, as I ran out on the field. The roar of the half-dozen four hundred and fifty horsepower Libertys fairly shook the earth, and their propellers send clouds of dust swirling upward. As I approached the line, a car tore into the airdrome. There was Shirley, her hair blowing in the wind, as she streaked down the road toward the ships.

As I got closer, I saw her fling herself out of the roadster and make a beeline for none other than Kennedy. Penoch O'Reilly was standing near by, his face a study.

"Kennedy going down?" I asked him, noting meanwhile that Shirley and Kennedy were holding hands.

"Begged to," boomed O'Reilly. "He's got guts, all right, and a craving for excitement."

"How's he acting—toward you, I mean?"

"Doesn't speak. Hardly speaks to anybody. I think he's afraid some of the rest are wise to him."

Just then I saw Shirley lean forward, as if to kiss him good-by. He looked around almost furtively and held her off. Mr. Ralph Kennedy, for the moment, was very unsure of his ground. As Penoch and I passed him on our way to our ships, his eyes rested on us for just a moment. They were passionless, but when his face was serious the meanness in it seemed to be intensified. Funny what an effect eyes too close together can give. Add that mouth—and my imagination—and perhaps you can see what I mean. Somehow, I shivered.

A moment later I was in my ship, giving her the last look-over, as she strained against the wheel-blocks. Oil pressure, air pressure, rotations per minute, battery-charging rate, temperature—all were O. K. Captain Kennard was already swinging out on the field; I being Number Two followed him, and the others took up the parade in their proper positions. One by one we took off, circling the field for altitude in single file. At a thousand feet the C. O. zoomed, and I slid in, twenty-five feet behind him, twenty-five feet to one side, and ten feet higher than he. Tex MacDowell came in on the left, and the others followed, until a V of ships, three on one side and four on the other, turned eastward and thundered their way toward the Gulf.

Formation is tricky stuff. You hold your position by throttle-handling alone. There are no brakes on airplanes, as you may have heard. It's no time to commence mooning upon the whichness of the what, nor the why of the how. You 'tend to your knitting, if you don't want a collision, and I 'tended to mine plenty. Subsconsciously I noted that Kennedy, at the rear of the left side, was holding his position well. Pretty fair flyer, he was. Penoch was behind me.

In an hour we were on the outskirts of the flood district. Ten minutes later I was stealing looks at the ground. We seemed to be flying over a shallow lake, from which houses and barns and cattle protruded. About two feet of water, I should say, covered the ground, and dozens of people were gathered on each knoll. Houses were down here and there, but not until we reached the outskirts of Laguna itself, did the real devastation become apparent.

As we circled that town, it seemed as if I couldn't move. It looked like some gigantic canvas, whereon some artist had painted his idea of a shambles. The back part of the town still had buildings; the streets, clogged with small débris and overturned automobiles, was the sole evidence, save for broken chimneys, of the water. The beach section was nothing but one gigantic rubbish pile. Ten-story buildings had toppled and fallen in ruins, and for a space of at least a square mile, it seemed, there was not even a lane through the wreckage. Try to picture a heap of rubbish, so gigantic that a hundred automobiles, or more, flung upon it looked like so many flies. Dozens of boats, ranging from oil-tankers to canoes, had been flung hundreds of feet inland, like so many children's toys flung on a dump.

The Gulf itself held a scum of débris of all kinds, and its shore, as far as we could see, was a rim of ruins.

I had not seen a single spot where a landing was possible. Kennard had wigwagged his ship, and one by one we fell into single file. Down below, thousands of people—the survivors—had their heads turned upward. Down in the ruins I could see bodies, now, and out in the bay unnumbered corpses were floating.

Suddenly Kennard started down, and then I saw what had been done. There had been other disasters and floods in Texas, when the airplanes had saved lives. Laguna had prepared. A force of hundreds of men was just finishing the job of clearing a hundred-foot runway down the hard-packed beach on the outskirts of the town; and it was there, one by one, that we landed, to face haggard, hollow-eyed men, steeped in tragedy.

Much happened during our days at Laguna; but that has nothing to do with Penoch O'Reilly and Ralph Kennedy. Anyway, twenty minutes later we were all back in the air, carrying packages of food and water, put up to float. Each of us had a sector assigned. We went roaring out over the open Gulf, spotting survivors who were floating on improvised rafts or clinging to planks. Kennard's ship, with Jack Beaman at the radio key, was flashing information to San Antonio. Soon the Donovan ships would be coming in, carrying supplies.

As we got out over the water, I turned to look at George Hickman, pointing downward. He's big and blond and nerveless; but his face was strained, and there was the closest thing to fear, that I've ever seen in his eyes.

As for me, I was one jump ahead of a fit. Down below, flashing along between carcasses of human beings and animals, were what seemed like untold hundreds of fins, cutting the water and feeding on their prey. Six times we swooped low to drop food and water to those poor wretches down below us. We could almost look into sharks' eyes, and time after time the flash of a white belly announced another mouthful.

Remember this, too. If we came down in the water, we could float two hours. There was not a single serviceable boat to rescue a soul.

I flew six solid hours that day, as did every one of the others. It was just before the last patrol, and getting dusk, when I ran into Kennedy for the first time. Our landings hadn't synchronized before.

"God!" I heard him mumble in an unutterably tired voice. "This'll drive me nuts! I can't even swim, if I come down."

"No difference, my boy," Jimmy Jennings told him with an attempt at jauntiness. "None of us could swim over a mile. Who thinks he could make five hundred feet through that forest of fins?"

And he was right. It seemed as if every shark in the Atlantic ocean had come to the picnic. But there were still unexplored sections, little towns along the shore which needed help, and on we went. Twenty Donovan ships were ferrying supplies; one came in almost every ten minutes. God knows we were willing to fly until we dropped. Those poor devils down in the water will haunt me to my dying day, I guess.

The sun was setting, when I turned around from a spot ten miles out in the Gulf, my last package dropped and my patrol over. My twelve-cylinder Liberty had never missed a lick, and I remembered saying over and over to the rhythm of the motors:

"If you'll only keep it up—if you'll only keep it up—"

My ears were ringing from a day's bombardment; my face was so sun-burnt with sun and wind that it was sore as a boil, and I was more tired than I've ever been in my life. Two other D.H.'s, one a mile to my right and the other on beyond, were coming home across the vile, befouled water.

I was two thousand feet high, and land was six or seven miles ahead, when Hickman grabbed me with a grip like a vise. My heart did a backflip, and I turned as if I'd been shot. He was pointing to the right. In a second I had swung my ship and was flying wide-open toward that middle D.H.

It was coming down in a shallow dive. The propeller was turning as slowly as a water-wheel. One look was enough to tell me that the motor was dead, and that only the air-stream was moving the stick.

Two of the boys were going to the sharks.

I was diving now, motor full on. I don't know why. I guess I had some wild idea that I could help them out. The other ship was heading for the falling D.H., too. We ranged alongside it almost together. The pilot in the crippled plane was Ralph Kennedy. The man in the third ship was Penoch O'Reilly.

Everyone was flying alone, except me, for two reasons. One was to leave more room for supplies to drop; the other was to conserve manpower as much as possible. I had George along to work the radio. We'd reconnoitered some outlying towns on the trip.

It seemed a year before the ship hit, and I was thinking at top speed, searching for some possible method of saving Kennedy. He could float for two hours; then he'd be sunk—

Just before the ship hit the water I let out a wild yell, which I myself couldn't hear. Right ahead of Kennedy was a huge, partially submerged thing floating. It looked like a bunch of logs tied together. I guess he never saw it.

The ship crashed into it with its undercarriage. Just what happened I don't know, because the water rose in a geyser, and I couldn't see for a moment. But what I saw, when the water subsided, was plenty.

It seemed that the ship had been crumpled completely. It had turned on its back. Kennedy was invisible. The fuselage had broken in half, the wings crumpled back, and the motor, of course, was under water. That little heap of wreckage would become water-soaked in a few minutes. It would sink in a quarter of an hour, instead of in two hours.

I guess I was shaking a little. I remember Penoch, circling and circling. Kennedy had not come to the surface.

"Knocked out and drowning—maybe a mercy," I was thinking, and four fins, circling, sent cold chills up and down my back.

Then he came to the surface. He struggled weakly to climb up out of the water, but it took him a full two minutes. Even then he was partly submerged. Suddenly the sight of those fins set me crazy, I guess.

"I'll give him a chance to drown, at least!" I fairly shouted at them; and the next second I was pouring machine-gun bullets into the shadowy green monsters, and they were floating, dead, on the surface of the water.

There was not one single, solitary thing that could be done to save him. Two minutes more, and his frail life-raft would be sunk. There was no time to fly back and get something to which he could cling and drop it to him. He couldn't swim.

I fairly froze in my seat, as a great mass of water rose from the sea. As it cleared, I saw the tail of Penoch's DeHaviland, high in the air, less than ten feet from Kennedy. The next second Penoch was clambering up on the wreckage of his own ship. A few seconds later he was stripped to his underwear, and swimming toward the crippled Kennedy.

As the little devil was towing his enemy I came to myself. I circled watchfully above the water, and machine-gunned an approaching shark. As I did that my stunned brain got working. I don't think I'm either better or worse than the average. I'm franker, that's all. If I had been sitting in my ship, while my deadly enemy was dying a sure death, I would have been conscious of a sense of relief.

Penoch O'Reilly had landed to give him two hours more of life; it seemed a certainty that at the end of two hours, Penoch, too, would go down to the sharks, with the man who had almost ruined his life.

Then and there that squat, little figure, ho-ho-ho-ing at life, grew into a giant, towering above ordinary mortals, as far as I was concerned.

"There must be some way," I kept telling myself over and over as I circled them. Maybe I hypnotized myself into an idea. I gave a war-whoop of relief. Anything was better than one hundred per cent. hopelessness.

Kennedy was hurt. That was apparent. Penoch had to drag him up on the fuselage, and then the reserve man lay there as if he were completely out.

I made wild motions to Penoch; he nodded. He was standing up, a small white figure, his feet far apart to brace himself against what fate had in store. As I sped for land, I almost thought I could hear him laughing that deep-toned, Rabelaisian laugh, flinging his challenge to the gods, a small white speck in the dusk.

A moment after I had landed, I'd told my story. Tex MacDowell and Sleepy Spears were in their ships in two seconds less than nothing, and we were off. When we arrived, Penoch had the upper left wing detached, and Kennedy was on it.

From there O'Reilly started his heartbreaking journey, a full mile, pushing that wing slowly through the water, his legs kicking tirelessly. Kennedy, partially recovered, was using the vertical fin as a paddle to help. Three airplanes cruised round and round over the ugly water, and not a shark got within our lines. Every second was a strain, for the sharks could come up from below and get Penoch, but they did not. With so much dead meat in the sea, I guess our outfit was entirely too suspicious for them to bother with.

It was ten minutes after dark when Penoch and Kennedy staggered up on the beach. Kennedy collapsed. When I got out of my plane, I was swaying like a rubber lamp-post, and before Penoch had been taken care of and got back, I had eaten and fallen on a cot, fully dressed, but dead to the world.

Strange as it may seem, I didn't see either of them next day. Our flyings came at different hours, and when one was on the ground the others were in the air. And at three in the afternoon, when I landed, I found that Penoch and Kennedy and Pete Miller had started back for McMullen. Kennard, Sleepy and Tex and I started home at five o'clock. There were Donovan ships available, and there'd been another bandit raid in our territory. The patrol was needed on the river.

I saw Penoch in the mess-hall, at dinner, and sat next to him. We were all ready to drop, and hadn't even washed. Kennard went to sleep over his soup. Sleepy Spears gave up after the meat course, and stumbled out to bed.

"Where's Kennedy?" I asked Penoch.

"In at Shirley's—for dinner," he said tersely and, as our eyes met, I guess our thoughts were the same.

"Then what you did for him had no effect, eh?" I finally asked him. "How'd he act?"

"Avoids me."

"I see. Come clean, Penoch. It must have been a temptation to leave him down there, even if you figured you'd have a good chance of saving him."

Penoch buttered some bread thoughtfully.

"I just couldn't; and I'd never thought of that wing gag. Just had an idea that there ought to be some way out—"

"So you tossed a few sharks right out of your mind, eh?" I interrupted.

"Oh, hell, I didn't think of anything, except how nice it would be if he was dead. Well, old-timer, he's sure slapped me in the face tonight by going back there. Shows what he is. Hell, I've been doing things for him all my life, and he's willing to blackmail me. Guess I was a damn' fool back over the Gulf, eh? Well, there'll be excitement about in a few days, I guess. Better get some sleep tonight. Ho-ho-ho!"

I knew then that he had fully made up his mind, that he'd considered everything, and was ready to go. And when that crisis was passed with Penoch O'Reilly, he feared not man, devil or circumstances. Right at that moment he figured that the Army was a thing of the past and that the world was waiting to be bucked by a man in disgrace. The tougher it was, the louder he'd laugh.

The next day we both saw Kennedy at breakfast. He greeted us with a straight stare, said, "Hello," in his customary breezy manner, ate with relish, and was absolutely himself. His eyes were as cold a green as ever, except for that surface shine that came when he laughed. He told a good story about Noah and the Johnstown flood, indulged in his reminiscences of the Columbus raid and likewise the Galveston flood, in all of which he had participated with considerable gusto.

I just sat there and watched him. That clear-cut, hard face and those fishy eyes made as impenetrable a mask as I've ever seen.

"The hell it's a mask!" I finally told myself. "He just hasn't any feelings that can't be expressed in a grin or a laugh or a snarl. He couldn't hate anybody real hard any more than he could like anybody very much. Except himself."

At lunch he came breezing in with:

"Well, well, the good old feedbag'll be fastened round my snoot pronto. The meal ain't been cooked that I can't clean up by myself."

He shook out his napkin, grasped his fork firmly and started in at the salad. His eating was not a pronouncedly delicate proceeding. It was audible for miles around when he wasn't trying to act unnaturally elegant; and I believe that in a straight contest Kennedy's eating anything could drown out my snoring.

"By the way, Peewee, my lad, how about a bit of poker at Shirley's Old Man's house tonight? I was given instructions to ask you and Slim to come out. Sheriff Trowbridge'll be there, too. Come, and bring your checkbook, because it's my night to howl!"

Penoch just looked at him. Kennedy stared back with a mirthless smile.

"Risk a few nickels!" he gibed. "I ain't seen your game for years. How about it? Shirley'll be glad to see you both, she said. She ain't had much time—"

"Yes, I'll go."

Simple, those words. But I knew as surely as I knew that I was at the table that Penoch's deliberate interruption was a threat. He stared straight at Kennedy, and the implication in his statement was plain for me to see. That poker game that night was to include some unscheduled fireworks. Shirley and her father were to hear some hitherto unknown episodes in the lives of Ralph Kennedy and Percival Enoch O'Reilly.

"Fine! A good time'll be had by all," Kennedy came back. "You act as though you'd been invited to risk your life, or attend your own funeral. Heh-heh-heh! Didja hear him say that, boys? Peewee don't think any more of a nickel lost at cards than he does his left eye."

There he sat, gibing at the man who had saved his life. It was apparent to any one that there was a deadly undercurrent in the conversation between the two. I saw Kennard and Tex and the others looking at them speculatively.

Directly after the meal I put it up to Penoch.

"You're going to lay your information on the line tonight, eh?" I asked him.

"Right. And my resignation'll be written. He doesn't intend to back away from Shirley. I can see that. Maybe what I say won't change a thing; but she'll go into it with her eyes open."

"Damn' funny, at that," I said in considerable bewilderment. "I don't see why a girl—any girl—could mean so much to Kennedy that he's willing to run the risk of exposure as a criminal. I—"

"He doesn't think I'll go through with it," rasped Penoch. "Well, I'm going to take a nap."

He strode away, his short legs twinkling through the dust, toward his tent. He didn't sleep, though, because I peeked in a few times. He wrote reams of letters, setting his house in order, as it were, before he moved out. And he didn't seem so downcast. In fact, the devil-may-careness of his face had increased, and there was hard recklessness there. He had taken his hundredth knockout blow from fate; and he was still standing erect, unbeaten.

It was a long and tough afternoon for me. Kennedy flew a patrol, and then took a long time dressing for dinner. At the meal he was in excellent form, holding the floor continuously with ribald tales, which were good. And Penoch O'Reilly, his eyes bright, seemed strung to a high nervous pitch. His roaring "Hoho-ho!" rolled forth continuously, and he and his enemy fought a silent battle of eyes beneath the laughter. I was depressed and silent, but possessed with such infinite hatred and repulsion when I thought of Kennedy that I could have stuck the bread-knife in his throat and enjoyed it.

I felt as if I were riding deliberately into disaster, when we went to the Curran house. Sheriff Trowbridge, Gargantuan old-timer, who had been friend and aid to the flight since its inception, was already there.

He was six feet two, with a shock of iron-gray hair, a great mustache, and a genial old face tanned to mahogany. He and Mr. Curran had been friends for years and, as we came up on the porch, Mr. Curran yelled in stentorian tones—

"Three new customers, sugar!"

He was tall and thin and bald, with piercing eyes and an aquiline nose, all of which gave him the appearance of a soft-hearted old eagle.

In a moment Shirley came out, bearing three long, cold drinks. Her eyes were on Kennedy. When I saw the smile on her lips and the look in those eyes, I sort of caught my breath. I don't know much about love, but almost anybody can recognize it when it stares them right in the face.

She was all in white, her golden hair slicked back, throwing her features into bold relief. Slim and lithe and tall, she looked every inch a thoroughbred. Kennedy, as he bent over her, was a good-looking officer, too. You couldn't see those mean eyes, in profile.

"And women are supposed to have intuition!" I groaned.

At that, there was a sort of new note in Kennedy's smile—a trace of real feeling—when he looked at her; and his eyes were a little less hard, maybe.

But the adulation was principally on her part. From the time the game started he seemed to avoid even looking at her. He played quietly, as did everybody. Every man around that table was a lover of poker and a hater of conversation when the pasteboards were being wooed. Even Shirley had had it bred in the bone, I guess, and never said a word. She tended to the ash receivers, brought us drinks, and finally went out on the porch to throw a ten-minute sop to a boy friend who had called on her.

The game was twenty-dollar take out, table stakes, and either draw or stud, to be played at the option of the dealers. Penoch watched Kennedy like a hawk, and so did I, on general principles. Not that I really thought he'd try his tricks there.

The most amazing thing to me was his utter nonchalance. He knew what Penoch was going to do before the evening was over; and he grinned into the little flyer's face and dared him with his eyes.

It was close to ten o'clock, and I was about fifty dollars ahead, Penoch even, and Kennedy sixty dollars winner. We'd been taking the two old-timers over the jumps, to our great glee and their humorous disgust.

It was Kennedy's deal. He shuffled them, and I saw him casually put an ace on the bottom before he started. When he finished, he gave the cards a rapid double cut—bottom half of the deck placed on top, but a little forward of the other half of the deck. Then he simply cut again, and that little shelf between the two halves of the deck enabled him to replace the cards exactly. That is, after two cuts, the cards lay exactly as they had before he'd cut them, the first time.

It was my cut, and he did not offer it, but started dealing.

My eyes were busy from that moment on. My heart was pounding as I visualized the possibilities. Maybe I could get Penoch out of the mess.

Card after card fell. Kennedy was high, with a king showing, and held the bet until the fourth card had dropped, when Sheriff Trowbridge drew an ace. I stayed, and Kennedy raised ten dollars. That dropped Penoch and Mr. Curran. The sheriff came back with a thirty-dollar re-raise, and I, with a pair of fours, dropped and devoted myself to watching. Had that cut been an accident? If it hadn't, how had Kennedy stacked them for himself? Or did his crookedness merely include the placing of one lone ace to use if necessary?

He came back with a fifty-dollar raise—his stack. The sheriff, who had bought four times already and had plenty of chips in front of him, saw the raise.

Every eye was concentrated on Kennedy. I was peering so hard it hurt, and somehow my mouth felt dry. Shirley came in, her eyes widening at the size of the pot. She stood back of Kennedy, without saying a word. I knew that she comprehended the hands perfectly—

the sheriff with ace, queen, ten showing; Kennedy with king, queen, deuce.

Slowly Kennedy flipped the sheriff's card. A seven. Kennedy studied his own hand a moment, and his eyes flickered around the table, a curious light in them. Suddenly he dealt. An ace! And from the bottom of the deck, so clumsily done that any one in the world could have caught it.

"Pair of aces!" he crowed, showing his hole card.

The silence was like a physical substance, throbbing and heavy and packed with evil. My eyes rested on Shirley's face. Her eyes were wide and horror-stricken, and she looked as if she were about to scream.

Suddenly the silence was shattered by the blow of Curran's fist on the table. As if it had set a spring into action, every man around that table, except Kennedy, was on his feet.

"Out of this house, you thieving, yellow, sneaking crook!" thundered the old man furiously. "There ain't a man here didn't see you take that ace from the bottom! Git out, I tell you, or I'll—"

He choked with his own wrath, as he crouched as if to leap across the table.

Kennedy got up leisurely, his eyes hard enough to make one's flesh crawl. They held an expression that I can not describe, but this I was sure of, crazy as it seemed—there was no rage in them. Perhaps he couldn't feel deeply enough to wax furious. It was as if he were dead.

"I guess you caught me," he said evenly.

He pulled down his blouse and ran his hand through his hair. Penoch was like a statue. Not one sound broke the stillness.

Then there came a strangled sob from Shirley. She rushed from the room, and from somewhere in the hall, before she got out of earshot, we heard her weeping.

I licked my lips with my tongue. I saw Curran's face twitch, and such demonaic fury leap into his eyes that I was afraid of murder. I believe he'd have sprung at Kennedy in another second.

"Sorry. Good night," Kennedy said slowly, almost as if he were playing a part.

He walked out without haste, and without a word or a look to any one of us.

"God! I'm sorry!"

Penoch's deep bass seemed to reverberate from the walls. As the sheriff broke into deep curses, Penoch interrupted him.

"Please, Sheriff, let me get this off my chest. Maybe you'll be through with me, now, too."

They sank into their chairs, Mr. Curran wiping his brow with a shaking hand. As Penoch made a clean breast of his relationship with Kennedy, I half listened, but I didn't pay close attention at that. A thousand crazy ideas were running through my head, and suddenly it seemed as if I couldn't wait to get Penoch alone. I had a queer hunch.

Those old-timers understood the little flyer's position, and the sheriff summed up the general sentiment, when he put his hand on Penoch's shoulder and told him:

"Mike, here, and me, ain't blamin' you a bit, son. And you was ready to prevent any trouble. You couldn't be blamed, any way you take it, for givin' him the benefit of the doubt for a while. Gosh! What a snake in the grass he is! And I aim to git him in jail. We'll plaster him for life—"

"And me with him," barked O'Reilly.

"Not a bit of it. Say, young feller, he can go up for a long time right in this country for what he done! More'n he deserves for this trick; but we'll sort o' consider his other crimes, see?"

"Listen Sheriff," I found myself saying. "Some way or another I've got a funny idea. Let me talk it over with Penoch and call you back, eh?"

The leonine old man peered at me through puckered eyes.

"Shore," he commented. "But what's the secret?"

"I'll tell you when I'm sure of it myself," I told him. "Good night, Mr. Curran. I sure hope Shirley won't take it too hard."

"She will, for awhile. But when I think o' what might 'a' happened if he hadn't give himself away—say, I ought to be thankful for this night!"

We had no sooner got out the door and into the car than I said:

"Don't start her for a minute. Penoch, my boy, just how good it was, or ought to be Kennedy with his fingers and a deck of cards?"

"Used to be a wonder!"

"And he deliberately, before five people, does the clumsiest piece of cheating a man ever did in the world! If he'd wanted to be caught, he couldn't have done it more openly."

"By God!"

It was almost a prayer from Penoch. Then he faced me, tense and strained, and his attempted whisper couldn't have been heard more than a hundred feet.

"He couldn't have done it deliberately! I know what you think—that because of what I did for him at Laguna he decided to give up Shirley and took that way. But all he had to do was walk out on her, without putting himself in disgrace."

"Let's talk to him," I suggested, and we started immediately to make a new speed record between McMullen and the flying field.

It did seem ridiculous. For what possible reason, short of sheer insanity, would a man brand himself a card-cheat? A man who'd do that would cut off his head to cure an earache. I couldn't make head nor tail of it, but I was exuding curiosity in corpulent chunks. I aimed to get at the bottom of things, and quickly.

We found him in his tent, alone, holding communion with a large bottle of tequila.

He stared at us, as we came in, and I'll swear his eyes brought me up short. There was suffering in them, and a sort of bewilderment. It changed the whole aspect of the man. It was his eyes that repelled one, ordinarily. Now that there was something human in them, the change was magical.

Penoch O'Reilly planted himself, as per usual, his mustache turned upward belligerently, and his eyes snapping.

"Regardless of anything else, Ralph, how the 'ell did you happen to cheat so clumsily? The cheating I can understand; the way it was done I can't."

Kennedy took a big drink, gave us one and, as he poured them, said sardonically:

"You give me credit for knowing better, then? You ought to."

"If you did it deliberately, why?" I broke in. "If you wanted to do what Penoch asked, and lay off the girl—"

"We both happened to be in love," he said calmly, as if laughing up his sleeve. His eyes, however, were averted.

"Huh?" snorted Penoch scathingly. "You in love?"

"For the first and only time in my life," Kennedy admitted casually, his back toward us. "In fact, I'm so nuts about her that I couldn't let her in for what she'd be in for with me. Don't flatter yourself, Peewee. It wasn't for you I did it. It was for her."

"But why that way?" I barked.

"If I just broke off," he said, eying a new glass of tequila with narrowed eyes, "she'd have taken a long while to get over it. Might as well cut everything off clean, show her what I am all at once, and blackjack her into hating me. Make it easier all around."

For a moment his eyes met mine, and the mask was off. I don't get sentimental as a rule, but I was looking at a man whose whole life had come up to torture him, and who was going through an accumulation of suffering.

"By the way, Peewee, I'm resigning, of course, and leaving tomorrow on the five o'clock. Probably'll have to borrow some dough. I'd like to take a last ride, so keep things quiet until I get it, eh?"

Penoch nodded wordlessly. Cocky as he was ordinarily, and sure of himself, he was nonplussed now. Kennedy had turned into a strange species of animal to him, and he couldn't believe it.

"And now," grinned Kennedy, keeping up his bluff to the last, "will you two get the hell out of here and let a gentleman and a scholar get drunk in peace and quiet?"

"Don't want any company?" Penoch asked him, and there was real pleading in his tone.

For the first time in our acquaintance I saw actual softness in Kennedy's eyes, as he looked at the man he had liked and admired as much as it had been possible for him to feel those emotions for anybody.

"Nope. Let's shuck the past, eh what? What the hell? And I've got to do a little high-powered thinking. 'Night."

We walked thoughtfully out into the starlight. Then I made a profound remark.

"I've heard of the miracles that love is supposed to work, but this is the first one I've seen. I think the combination of you risking your life for him, and a real unselfish feeling for a girl, has sort of opened up a new world to Kennedy. He's got guts, hasn't he?"

"Never lacked those," boomed Penoch. "At that, you may be right. I guess he's always figured every hand was against him—and now that he's found out there's a little white in the world he doesn't know what to make of it. He proved himself, all right, tonight, but if he'd told me that this afternoon I'd have laughed as hard as I would over a romantic yarn about the honeymoon of a salmon."

"'Night. I don't feel much like talking."

To tell the truth, I didn't either. I wandered around the field, smoking a few reflective cigarets, and finally called up the sheriff. I told him the whole story, and he was satisfied that everything pointed to the fact that if he didn't make a move everything was all right. I figured it was better, and so did he, that Shirley should never know the inside. Consequently, the Currans were not called up, and have not had the real dope to this day.

I finally went to sleep, but in the morning I was, of course, still thinking about one Ralph Kennedy. And for some funny reason I wasn't sure of him—his sincerity, I mean. I was wondering whether there wasn't some trick connected with his gesture of the night before. However, I thought it best, at breakfast—to which meal he did not lend his presence—to tell the boys the entire yarn, simply to offset the gossip that would run wild around McMullen. Mr. Curran, of course, would eventually spill the beans, and I wanted the gang to speak up, knowing the facts, and say whatever they deemed best. Furthermore, I had a funny idea that when Kennedy left, I didn't want him to go in disgrace.

As the day wore on, I came to think more and more of this last flight stuff. All flyers are more or less superstitious about that. As a matter of fact, there have been a few, from Hobey Baker down, who've met their Waterloo on the last hop before they kissed the Air Service good-by. I had a sort of premonition that it shouldn't be taken.

Consequently, when Kennedy ate bacon and eggs at lunch, with his eyes red, a hang-over sticking out all over him, I said:

"Listen, big boy, you've said you were leaving tonight and likewise that you were going to take a last jazz flight. You were drunk as a hoot owl last night, and I don't think you'll be in such good shape to fly this afternoon. Why not douse the idea of a hop?"

"Maybe you've got a good idea there," he said with a grin that didn't change the suffering eyes. "In fact, it's probably the good old logic. Say, Peewee, how about you taking me for a ride, so nothing'll happen?"

"Sure. I'll go with you."

I just happened to switch my gaze from one to the other, and I saw something. There were many experiences that they had gone through together in the past, which, naturally, had generated a certain feeling between them. But now each of them had discerned something in the other that transcended anything that they had previously known.

In short, I saw a man's affection for another man shining from each pair of eyes.

The rest of the gang, knowing the entire situation, chimed in with a lot of Air Service kidding, about that last ride, as for instance, Sleepy Spears' remark:

"Any hop is foolish, and a last one is suicide. You've made it sure death by letting Penoch fly you."

"In fact," Tex MacDowell chimed in, in his soft southern drawl, "I've had a shovel all ready to pick Penoch up with, for a long time. I'd pick a hang-over in preference to Penoch any time."

I guess nobody outside of the men who fly understand what air kidding is. Probably I don't myself. But in my dumb way I think that it's like a kid's whistling when he passes a graveyard, or, perhaps, laughing at the worst that could happen, so that, when it does happen, it won't mean anything.

When lunch was over, and we were all drifting out of the mess-hall, I suddenly realized that I would like to share, a little bit, those last hours. I'd been so close to the thing that I wanted to hang around the outskirts of it, until Kennedy left. In other words, I was sentimental, and I thought quite a lot of Penoch, at that. So I said casually—"I think I'll take a little private hop for myself when you do—a sort of chaser for the poker game, eh?"

Kennedy, I think, bewildered as he was at the world that had been opened to him so recently, appreciated the impulse behind my suggestion.

"Sort of be my guard of honor, eh?" he said. But those cold eyes were soft. "In fact, we'll be glad to have company, won't we Peewee?"

And so it happened that a half-hour later the three of us were on the line. Our two ships were being warmed up, and the mechanics, satisfied, had brought them down to idling.

"I'll sit in the back seat, big boy," Penoch told Kennedy, "but don't think that I won't take the stick away from you any time!"

You know, of course, that De Havilands are dual-control ships, but all the instruments are in the front cockpit, and that, in a manner of speaking, is the driver's seat.

I got into my own plane and, as I taxied out for the take-off, I couldn't exactly analyze my reason for being there. I guess it was a sort of vague tribute to Kennedy, and yet I had a funny feeling that something might happen—so much so that as I turned the motor full on and pushed the stick forward I was so absent-minded that I nearly broke the propeller, because I had the nose of the plane down so far.

Kennedy and Penoch had taken off first, and I just followed them as they circled the field for altitude. When we got to the tremendous height of fifteen hundred feet, Kennedy, who was doing the piloting, started due west for Laredo.

I'll swear that we were not a thousand yards from the airdrome when it happened. I was flying possibly a hundred yards back of them, and almost the same distance to the right. All of a sudden I saw their ship go into a dive.

That meant something. When Kennedy started turning back toward the field I knew that the motor had cut out. Then, as I noticed the propeller, I knew that the motor had not only cut out, but had cut dead. The stick was revolving slower and slower. There was no motor power behind it.

The next second their ship was blanketed in fire. The motor was a mass of blue flame. Kennedy had not cocked the ship up into a side-slip soon enough. That blows the flames upward, away from the pilot. The left wing was afire before he started slipping, and that second of backward draught, because they were in a dive when the fire started, had caused the fuselage to catch fire in a dozen places.

My body and brain were numb. Even so, I subconsciously knew what had happened. The gas line had broken, and the gas, sprayed over the hot motor, had ignited.

They had gone into the slip—too late—before I started toward them. I was diving my ship, motor full on. There was nothing I could do—Penoch and Kennedy burned to death before my eyes—I was just getting nearer for no reason.

I suppose that it registered on me at the time, because I remember it so vividly now. Penoch told me what was said. Anyway, I saw Kennedy, bearing the brunt of the fire in the front cockpit, turn and gesture. He was talking. I could see through the smoke and fire his lips moving. Penoch told me that what he said was:

"Get out on the wing! I'm not leaving the ship— Let me jump! If Slim sees you, he'll get close. God! I can't last long! It'll just be two instead of one—"

What I saw was Penoch getting out of the back cockpit, hanging by his hands from the cowling. He hauled himself along the side of the ship, his feet dangling over space. His head was turned backward, to protect his eyes, and his clothing was charring, because he was out where the air-stream could reach him, and no flame could get a real start. But Kennedy, in the cockpit—

I was going through the most horrible nightmare that can be conceived. And yet, I instinctively sensed the possibility of saving Penoch, as he reached the right wing and started crawling along it.

Then Ralph brought the burning ship level; that blew the fire right back on him. I was close, and for that horrible minute I guess I ceased to think of my own safety. I knew that there was one desperate chance to save one of the two, and Penoch, of course, was the one, because Kennedy had willed it so.

Penoch was out of the fire now, at the edge of the right wing. He was hanging from the edge of it by his hands as I flew my ship up into position, my left wing underneath the other's right one. And Kennedy—I don't know by what transcendent power he was able to do it, as he burned to death—kept his ship level. Penoch dropped—his only chance for life—and he landed on my left wing. He grabbed the cabane strut, the little metal horn at the edge of the wing to which the control wires for the ailerons are attached, and passed out.

An instant later, Kennedy, a human bonfire, leaped from his burning ship. He fell out—blessed surcease from pain. And the ship, like a flaming coffin, seemed to follow his body down.

Penoch eventually got back into the rear cockpit, of course, and we're both here to tell the tale.

Sometime I hope that a burning ship will cease to trace a crimson path across my dreams. Probably it won't.

Anyway, if Ralph is a spook in some spiritual village, teaching the Twelve Apostles how to play poker, I hope he has time to tip his halo in acknowledgment of the salute of Slim Evans to a crook and a hero, a scoundrel and a man.

The End